Sto[illegible] of Paradise

MARY OBOZUA

Hashtag PRESS

Published in Great Britain by Hashtag Press 2019

A CIP catalogue for this book is available from the British Library.

ISBN 978-1-9993006-5-4

Typeset in Garamond Classic 14/18.5 by Blaze Typesetting
Printed in Great Britain by Clays Ltd, St Ives plc

Hashtag PRESS

HASHTAG PRESS BOOKS
Hashtag Press Ltd
Kent, England, United Kingdom
Email: info@hashtagpress.co.uk
Website: www.hashtagpress.co.uk
Twitter: @hashtag_press

Dedicated to Tiwa Oyadare

Acknowledgements

Thanks to my Father, Dr Yaya and my mother, Cordelia Obozua, who have both encouraged me to put pen to paper. To my incredible siblings, Martha, Mishael, Ruth and Rachel, thank you for believing in me and for our honest love and support for each other. You make me thankful daily and I love you all so much.

To Ryan Smith. Your support for me and my wild ideas produce great things. I love you for that and I'm excited to see where this leads. . .

To Hashtag Press, I cannot thank you enough for bringing a dream into reality and teaching me so much. Thank you for responding to my email and for working with me tirelessly. To Helen Braid, thank you for the cover. I really do love it.

Once again, thank you to my amazing friends, who support me with such joy and enthusiasm.

Y'shua. Without you I'm truly just a dreamer. I love you more daily. Thank you for your endless love.

From the Author

To my fabulous friends who are more like sisters, this is for you! To the special ones who have inspired this book: Adesola, Edwina, Olamide & Christine; thank you for years of belly hurting laughter and moments that couldn't possibly be made up. You make my life thrilling and adventurous and this is the best way I can keep these memories alive.

I look forward to sharing these stories with your children, my nieces and nephews, children around the world and, one day, my own.

I hope those who read these stories will laugh as much as we do and will love each character, as they are inspired by real people–my friends and family. I owe this book to you all!

Lots of love,

Mary

Stars of Paradise

Welcome to Marshill, home to Daisy Denby, Ewe Acquah and their wonderful friends. Daisy and Ewe love to create new and exciting inventions on the Grape4Dimension computer that brings Ewe's drawings and Daisy's coding to life. With the Grape4D, quick wit and teamwork, these amazing kids can solve any problem that comes their way.

Prologue

The Missing Chalice

Three months ago

"Daisy! Get in here quickly!" Ewe yelled.

"Where are you?" shouted Daisy. "I can't see you anywhere."

Ewe was in the museum corridor, by the storeroom door. It was slightly ajar. Perfect! She quickly ducked in and frantically searched for Daisy. She could hear the other children and visitors in their tour group screaming and running down the corridors.

"Ewe?" Daisy said, sounding close by.

"I'm in here, to your left! In the storeroom."

"I can't see you!" Daisy cried.

Ewe could see Daisy looking worried, as her head swivelled from left to right. Daisy grabbed her arm and pulled her into the storeroom.

"I want to go home," Daisy said, looking close to tears.

The visitors participating in the museum tour of the Mystery Ancient Exhibition were running like headless chickens in all directions. Louis, their tour guide, wasn't much help. He had dropped his pile of brochures and maps on the floor, as he ran through the corridors, waving his hands in the air in a flurry.

"I can't believe this is happening to me," moaned Daisy, with her head in her hands.

"You? This is happening to everyone, so let's pull our socks up and figure something out," Ewe said, sounding more confident than she felt.

They were on a Marshill School Year Six trip to look at ancient artefacts and paintings. They had specifically come to see King Joseph's chalice.

The chalice was indeed a wonder; a silver goblet encrusted with jewels. It was locked away in a thick glass cabinet with a red laser light flashing in front of it.

"This chalice was once owned by King Joseph of Marshill," Louis explained to the children. "King Joseph went to invade a nearby city to retrieve this very chalice from an enemy who had stolen it from his father. Legend has it that when the chalice is filled with water, the one who drinks from it receives super human strength! King Joseph became the strongest King of all time, thanks to the chalice."

Daisy looked at Ewe and rolled her eyes. "It sounds like a fairy tale if you ask me."

It just so happened that this day and time was the perfect moment for Dirty Dexter to carry out the biggest heist in Marshill for a long time–stealing King Joseph's chalice. Dirty Dexter was always up to no good, stealing anything that sparkled.

"Can't you draw us out of this nightmare?" Daisy asked.

Ewe tried to find Daisy's face in the darkness of the storeroom. She could just about make out her big brown eyes that glistened against her brown skin.

"I need to draw something that will not just help us, but everyone else, to get away from Dirty Dexter and stop him from stealing the chalice. I have my Grape4D tablet with me in my backpack."

"Your tablet is just a miniature version of the real computer, right? So, you can only scan an existing thing and alter it?" Daisy asked.

"Yes, so think hard," Ewe said, taking off her backpack and pulling out her tablet.

Daisy huffed. "Doesn't this room have a light switch or something?"

Ewe rolled her eyes. "Of course there will be light! Try feeling around by the door, or the wall next to it, but don't open it. Keep it closed. We won't be in here much longer."

Daisy ran her hand around the walls until she felt a button. She pressed it and a dim light turned on above them.

"I really thought that was an old lady," Daisy said quietly.

Ewe laughed. "Sorry, I know it's not funny but what a disguise!"

Only a few minutes ago, Louis had been telling them more about the chalice. Daisy spotted, from the corner of her eye, an old lady hanging on to his every word.

How odd, Daisy had thought. She had never seen an old lady wearing black Doc Martins.

"Hello sir," the old lady had said, approaching Louis. "Did you just tell these children that whoever drinks from the chalice will receive super human strength?"

"Yes, I did, but I also said it's a myth, so believe it at your own peril!"

"But how do you know it's just a myth?" she asked curiously.

"Because it is madam," said Louis matter-of-factly. "If you want more information you can get a booklet from the help desk by the gift shop."

While Louis turned his attention back to the children, the old lady rubbed her chin, and walked closer to the chalice. The children gasped as she pressed her hand against the glass, leaving a small black button.

"What is she doing?" Ewe said. "No one is allowed to touch the glass."

"Look!" Daisy shouted, drawing Louis' attention–he looked like he was going to faint.

The old lady had ripped off her mask and pulled off her wig to reveal Dirty Dexter! He growled at the children making them scream and run for cover.

"The chalice is mine!" he declared.

He pressed a buzzer on a gadget in his hand, which made the black button vibrate.

SMASH!

The glass cabinet shattered into pieces. Dirty Dexter grabbed the chalice, took out a bottle from his coat pocket and tipped water into the shiny cup. He drank it down before he wiped the back of his mouth with his hand, looked up to the ceiling and roared, "GIVE ME THAT SUPER HUMAN STRENGTH!"

Suddenly, his whole body glowed. He balled his fists and began to run around the exhibition, grabbing the statues off the ground with a flick of a finger. It wasn't a myth! Dirty Dexter now possessed super human strength!

"I should have known something wasn't right when I saw the old lady's boots!" Daisy moaned, watching Ewe look around the storeroom.

Ewe was searching through the endless bottles of cleaning products. Some were for the bathroom; some were for the floor and some were for pests. Ewe grinned.

"Grab me that one." She pointed at a large cleaning product on the shelf beside Daisy.

Daisy picked it up and read the label. "Extremely Clean Dirt Exterminator, spray directly on pests."

"That will work. Dirty Dexter is the biggest pest of them all! Right, put it here so I can quickly scan it."

Ewe held her tablet a few centimetres away and ZAP! The inbuilt camera scanned the bottle and produced a high quality picture ready for Ewe to draw something that would change the purpose of the cleaning product and save the Marshill Museum.

"Look at this," Ewe tapped the tablet screen with her Touch Pen. Daisy peered a little closer over her shoulder. "It may not look like anything yet, but I'm drawing Dirty Dexter on the bottle behind a hazard sign. I'm changing the formula of the liquid to recognise Dirty Dexter as the target!"

"But we can't exterminate him because he has the chalice and all the other precious items. They'll be exterminated as well," Daisy said.

"Oh no, you're right," Ewe said frustrated.

"Wait! What about a net? If you alter the formula so that when we spray it on Dirty Dexter it turns into a really strong spider's web, it could hold him until we call the police. Pass me the tablet."

Ewe handed it over and Daisy typed in a code. She took another scan of the bottle before pushing the activation button.

A light shot out of the camera lens and hit the Extremely Clean Dirt Exterminator. It shook and bobbed around as though it were doing a dance.

Ewe grabbed the bottle. "Let's go get him."

The corridors were silent. The girls crept out of the storeroom and retraced their steps back to the exhibition. All the artefacts were scattered over the floor and Dirty Dexter was happily filling his pockets with jewels.

"Dirty Dexter, your time is up!" Ewe yelled.

He turned and growled at them. "I'm the strongest man alive. No one is going to stop me."

"Oh yeah?" Daisy placed her hands on her hips. "Let's see how strong you are after a good clean! Get him Ewe."

The spray shot across the room landing on Dirty Dexter. The liquid instantly hardened around him like a spider's web.

"Get this off me now!" he screamed.

"I'm going to find an adult to call the police," Daisy said, running off.

Ewe folded her arms and smiled. Dirty Dexter wouldn't be stealing anything again any time soon.

Chapter I

The Golden Invitation

A golden envelope popped through the letterbox of the Denby's house.

It was a typical Monday morning in May, when spring was reluctantly fluttering away, leaving room for summer to pleasantly tiptoe in.

School day mornings, however, were not as pleasant as the beautiful weather. Oh no! They were always busy, with the same chaotic rushing around the house to get ready.

The letter was addressed to 'Miss Daisy Lenora Denby of Class Six Everest' typed clearly in bold black ink. A small, white and gold, embossed stamp was neatly stuck to the far right corner of the envelope bearing the picture of the city

Mayor, Mr Over, dressed in a sharp purple suit with a crisp white shirt.

Every May, a golden envelope arrived at the home of every child at Marshill School. This could only mean one thing. The carnival was coming!

In the summer, Marshill hosted the biggest and most exciting carnival. This was the opportunity for the children of the town to enjoy a fantastic party, wear the best costumes, perform and win lots of prizes.

"Daisy, come downstairs quick!" called Alfred, Daisy's Dad.

Daisy was upstairs brushing her teeth.

"Uuh-cmmmm," she replied with a mouthful of toothpaste.

Alfred looked up the stairs. "What did you just say?"

Daisy spat out the toothpaste. "I said I'm coming Dad. What is it?"

"Come down and see. You're going to love it."

"Really?" Daisy asked excitedly.

"I'll tell you this much. A golden letter has arrived and it can only mean one thing."

Daisy shot out of the bathroom and jumped down the stairs two at a time.

"Careful Daisy," said Mitsy, Daisy's Mum, who had baby Faith balanced on her knees. "I've told you before how dangerous it is to jump down the stairs."

"Sorry," said Daisy, as she slowed down to a snail pace. "I'll walk like I'm balancing eggs on my head."

Mitsy laughed as she watched Daisy pretending to have a basket of eggs on her head.

"You can open it Dad," Daisy said. "I've been waiting for this since last year's carnival. What's the theme for this year?"

"Be patient, Daisy," said Alfred, as he opened the envelope.

Daisy's hair was tied in two bunches with red ribbon, which matched the little red bows on her black patent shoes. As she jumped up and down, her bunches jumped along with her.

Alfred pulled out the golden letter. Putting on his blue-framed glasses that always balanced on his head, he took a deep breath and began to read out loud, "Dear Daisy, you have been invited to the annual carnival. The theme for this year's carnival is birds of paradise!"

"Wow," exclaimed Daisy, then she frowned. "What are birds of paradise?"

"Birds of paradise are a collection of the most colourful birds on our planet," explained Mitsy. She stood to her feet and hoisted baby Faith on her hip, who was playing with her Mum's waist-length braids. "They live in exotic places and can transform themselves in a way that shows their colour and beauty. They often dance and make wonderful sounds. They really are magnificent!"

"Dance?" Daisy said surprised. Then she giggled to herself as she thought of a large, rainbow-coloured bird breakdancing.

"Ow!" Mitsy cried, as Faith pulled her braids hard and tried to squeeze them in her mouth.

Daisy laughed and helped her mum by moving the braids over her left shoulder away from her little sister's dribble-drenched mouth, as she babbled away. It looked like baby Faith was also excited about attending her first carnival!

"Thank you, darling," Mitsy winced as she wiped the dribble from her braids with a cloth. "I think it's playpen time now, Faith." She gently settled Faith into her playpen to merrily chew on her jelly toys. "Where were we?"

"You were telling me that birds of paradise are colourful. . . and they dance," Daisy said, eager to hear more.

"Oh yes! In fact, when I was younger, I went on holiday with some friends from university during our summer break. You remember Auntie Kate?"

"I love Auntie Kate!"

"She was part of the group that I went on holiday with. We went to an amazing garden centre where they had a bird sanctuary. We were able to see some of these special birds and learn about them. And yes, they really do dance and have very long, beautiful feathers."

"I love the idea of a dancing bird!" Daisy said excitedly. "Actually, a brightly coloured dancing bird! When we can start making the costumes?"

"We have two months until the carnival," said Mitsy.

"Two months!" Daisy moaned. Two months felt like forever!

"Why don't you have a chat with your friends and see what they're going to do for the carnival?"

"Good idea!"

"Before I go to work ladies, there's more to the letter," Alfred said. "It looks like Mr Over has added a challenge this year with a mystery prize."

He handed the letter to Daisy who read it out loud for her Mum to hear.

"This year we hope we will bring everyone together in a way we never have before. The carnival will have a singing contest with a mystery prize for the winners. Here are the rules: You must work together in a group. The group must make up a song together and they must also perform the song on the main stage." Daisy gasped. "Wow, I've never had to perform *anything* on stage before."

"That's why it's called a challenge," said Alfred. "I suppose it's something you and your friends can all work on together. Something that, for once, keeps you out of trouble." He gave Daisy a knowing look.

"Hey, we saved the town from Dirty Dexter, remember?"

"Adventurous Daisy," Mitsy shook her head. "I can't believe Fifi still has a neon green section of hair from one of your many adventures."

"That was a mistake!" Daisy argued.

"You have two months until the carnival, so there's plenty of time to work something out," Alfred said. "You and your friends will also have to focus and practice really hard, and think about what bird best represents you, so you can make great costumes. This is a perfect time to showcase your talents and hopefully win the mystery prize." Alfred glanced at his watch. "I've got to get to work. Be quick or you'll be late for school. I'll see you all this evening."

"Wait Dad!" Daisy shrieked, stopping him from walking quickly out of the front door. "My hoverboard doesn't work properly. I think Ewe needs to check the plans and draw it again. It's so slow that even a tortoise could beat me in a race."

Alfred laughed. "I'll drop you at school on the way."

"Bye Mum," Daisy said, running back to hug her. "Bye Faith." She waved at her sister who was too busy playing with her toys to notice.

"Have a fun day, sweetie," Mum replied.

Chapter 2

Who's A Little Birdie?

As Daisy walked through the school gates she noticed even more hustle and bustle than usual. Children from every year group were talking excitedly together. It was clear everyone had received the invitation to the carnival, as every now and then she could hear the words 'birds of paradise' buzzing in conversations around her.

Daisy ran past the groups of children straight into the school building. Registration was about to happen and she didn't want a detention. As she pushed open the doors to her classroom, Daisy stopped and took a deep breath. Class Six Everest had a makeover!

"Woah!" Daisy looked around the class in awe.

Class Six Everest usually looked like a normal classroom; grey tables with matching grey chairs grouped to fit six students per table, facing their teacher, Ms Tori. Behind Ms Tori's desk was the rainbow wall, where the best poems and paintings hung. Colourful desktop computers were at the back of the room. The machine that turned used waste paper into fresh, clean recyclable paper and the instant colour machine (that produced any colour ink you needed for the special pens) were at the back of the classroom.

But today, Ms Tori had decorated the classroom to look like a jungle, using paper moulds of exotic birds that looked so life-like; neon blues mixed with bright pinks. It was so thrilling to see the wonderstruck expressions of the other children walking around the room. The tables and chairs were no longer grey but decorated with foliage and sequins.

"Daisy!" Ewe, her best friend called out to her.

Although the classroom was flamboyantly decorated, Ewe stood out. She was wearing her favourite mint green t-shirt under her school shirt. Daisy thought no one pulled off mint green better than Ewe. The colour seemed to make her dark brown skin glow.

Daisy waved back and walked across to their table tucked in the corner.

"You're usually here first," Ewe remarked, as they hugged.

"My hoverboard doesn't work properly. Dad had to drop me off at the bottom of the hill."

"I'll take a look at my drawings after school and draw another one. How cool is this carnival? I feel excited and nervous all at the same time!"

"My Dad says this will be a good opportunity for us to focus on winning the show rather than getting into any trouble."

Ewe huffed. "Does no one remember that we saved the museum?"

Daisy laughed. "That's what I said. What do you think about this performance for the carnival? I've never even been on a stage before, let alone performed on one! Have you?"

"Nope," said Ewe, looking even more nervous. "Oh, look!"

Ewe pointed at their friends who walked into the classroom a minute before registration: Fifi, Danny and Ayo. The girls laughed as they saw their jaws drop at the incredible transformation of the classroom.

Ayo spotted them first and they all hurried over to Daisy and Ewe.

"Guess what happened?" Ayo said to Ewe. "None of our hoverboards work."

"Oh." Ewe smiled sheepishly. "Looks like all of them have to be fixed."

Before they could continue the conversation, Ms Tori walked in, dressed in a pink pencil skirt and blouse. It was exactly 8:45am and that meant it was time for registration with no talking or messing around. Everybody settled in their seats.

"Good morning class."

"Good morning Ms Tori," the class replied in unison.

"I'm sure you've all received your invites to the carnival this year. As you can see we have a wonderful theme–birds of paradise. All the classes have been decorated to give you lots of ideas to make your costumes. Now, after registration Mr Tony, our head of year, is coming by to talk to us about the birds and give us some inspiration to help with your performances."

There was an immediate flurry of questions.

"Do we all have to sing? Because I can't!"

"Will there be real birds at the carnival?"

"What's the mystery prize?"

"Class, I'm not going to tell you what the mystery prize is." Ms Tori stood up from her seat and walked across to the white board. "Or it wouldn't be a mystery, would it? I'll write down your questions on the board and go through them after registration. The carnival is one of the highlights of the year. Mr Tony will be here any minute, so let's get through the registration as quickly as possible, as we have something to show you. Anna?"

Ms Tori continued with the rest of the names while Mr Tony crept into the classroom dressed as a bird of paradise. The quiet classroom erupted with excited surprise and giggles.

"Wow! What is he wearing?" Daisy said.

"Is that really Mr Tony?" Ewe asked, squinting her eyes.

"Look at his shoes!" Ayo said and Danny laughed loudly.

Ms Tori clapped her hands. "Quieten down class. All will be explained soon. Please, let's get through the register. Now where was I? Wendy?"

Mr Tony's costume was very distracting, so it was hard for the class to pay attention. It was so bright and the feathers were huge! He was wearing yellow tights and brown shoes, and he was still wearing his glasses through the blue bird costume that covered his face.

"I think I know what type of bird he's dressed up as," Daisy whispered to Ewe.

Ewe looked back at Daisy with her eyes wide with anticipation.

"I think Mr Tony is a blue bird of paradise," replied Daisy confidently. "That's what I remember from the pictures around the room."

"The correct name is a Paradisaea Rudolphi," Fifi whispered. "Apparently, that bird is the loveliest of all male birds. Look! He even captured the blue bird's brilliant violet plumes."

"Why don't you just say feathers?" Ayo teased and Fifi nudged him.

Danny stared back at her in amazement. "How did you know that?"

"Well, I have this book at home all about types of birds and I also went online and–"

"Fifi, please be quiet," interrupted Miss Tori, looking cross.

"Sorry," Fifi said.

"Right, now that I have finished, Mr Tony is about to tell us a bit more about the carnival."

Mr Tony smiled. "Yes, indeed, there is a mystery prize up for grabs for the best performance and just in case you were wondering what type of bird of paradise I am, I'm the *Paradisaea Rudolphi.*"

Fifi winked at Daisy.

"Look around the room as I go through my presentation and see the pictures of the different types of birds I am speaking about. I want to make sure everybody gets the chance to learn, as well as have fun. I think it's best to show you something to inspire your performances. Ms Tori, hit the switch!"

Ms Tori pulled a little white tablet out of her drawer. There was a gentle whirling sound and suddenly the blank walls were filled with moving images of colourful party lights and flying birds of paradise. Funky music filled the room. It was like they had been transported to a live musical showcase!

Mr Tony pulled out a microphone from under the wing of his costume and handed it to Esmerelda Pendleton (everyone called her Esi).

Now, there's something you should know about Esi. She could really sing! However, petite little Esi was not very kind. Esi opened her mouth and her big bold voice echoed around the room; she sang about each bird as they popped on the screen.

When she was done, there was a moment of stunned silence, before the class let out a roar of applause.

"Come on class, let's spread great vibes all around. Esi came in early to work on this with us, just to show you all what you can do. I think she deserves another round of applause," Ms Tori said, looking proud.

Esi smiled smugly.

"I was actually super excited to do this show. I don't think that inspired me at all," said Fifi, crossing her arms.

"Ewe, can you draw me a voice like that?" Daisy asked.

"I wish!" said Ewe. "I need her voice desperately."

"Guys, how do we beat that?" Danny asked. "Surely Esi will do her own performance? And no doubt she will win as she always does!"

Fifi groaned. "What's the point of even trying?"

"But that's against the rules," said Ayo. "She can't sing by herself. The rules clearly state that we have to work in a group."

"Come on guys, yes, Esi was great, but if we think really hard and come up with a good performance that involves everyone, we have a good shot too," Daisy said.

"I agree," said Ewe. "We can all do great things. We can come up with something amazing. Ayo and Danny can breakdance and I know Esi can't."

"Ayo and Danny can choreograph a dance," Daisy suggested.

"Sure! But everyone needs to join in. No excuses this time." Ayo was looking at Fifi, who laughed in reply.

"Just don't make it too hard with lots of twists and spinning around on our heads. We can't actually breakdance!"

"I don't mind trying," said Daisy. "But I agree with Fifi. Let's stick to what we do best, so we can win that mystery prize and beat Esi."

"I want to be in charge of styling," said Fifi. "My big sister, Kim, is great at making clothes with her sewing machine, I can ask her to make the designs I create."

"We need to come up with a chart-topping song. Any suggestions?" Ewe asked.

No one volunteered. Singing was not their strong point.

"Right, we sort of have a plan," Ewe said. "Let's meet at my house after school and brainstorm."

After school, they made their way to Ewe's. Her house may seem normal from the outside;

however things always got a little interesting when you pressed the little button on the right-hand side of her bedroom door. . .

Chapter 3

Ewe's Room

The gang stood outside Ewe's bedroom door waiting to be let in. She had a fingerprint recognition device attached to the right-hand side of the door. It stopped her older sister, Grace, from messing around with her stuff. Ewe placed both thumbs on the scanner. It made a 'beep' sound and flashed green.

She leaned forward and said the password very slowly, "Strawberry jam." The door pinged open and they rushed in.

Ewe switched on her Grape4D desktop computer and the computerised voice said, "Welcome back, Ewe. Are you ready to draw?"

Ewe had begged her parents to buy her the

latest Grape4D computer, however it was very expensive and they didn't understand why she just couldn't use a regular computer. Thankfully, Ewe's Auntie Mabel understood and had got her the Grape4D for Christmas. It was the best computer ever! With the Grape4D, Ewe and Daisy were able to bring their illustrations to life and create cool things like the hoverboards.

The Grape4D was connected to a large glass case about four feet high that was attached to a mint green laser machine. Whatever Ewe drew, using her Touch Pen on her interactive mat, it would be projected on to the Grape4D, then Daisy could use her coding to perfect it. Once it was ready, it would pass through a tube and sketched out in 4D by the laser machine.

At this stage, everyone would need to wear a pair of black protective glasses so the laser would not hurt their eyes. Ewe would then press the black button on her computer that turned the 4D sketch into a real-life object. It would jerk backwards and forwards whilst the image formed.

Ewe was forever grateful to her Auntie Mabel.

She was Ewe's Dad's younger sister. Auntie Mabel told everyone she was an astronaut, but Ewe and Daisy knew she was a secret agent. Every now and then, Auntie Mabel called Ewe and Daisy to ask them for extra gadgets to help with her latest job. She even allowed them to visit her Secret Service Head Office. Daisy and Ewe couldn't wait to work there when they got older.

Ewe's room was like their own headquarters. They had a working lab, a gallery for all the artwork, prototypes and Ewe's beloved EWE-TUBE. The EWE-TUBE was an application Ewe had invented to watch their adventures on. It was always fun to see some of the things that happened and all the bloopers! Like that time when Daisy wore the bouncy trainers to play basketball, then bounced so high over the hoop, they thought she was going to end up in space!

Ewe was spinning round and round on her desk chair whilst her friends crammed onto her bed.

"Before I fix hoverboards, I think we should invent a drone camera to capture our performance, so we can watch it on the EWE-TUBE when we're finished," Ewe said.

"You mean a camera attached to a drone that can get all the angles of the stage?" Ayo asked.

"Exactly! But I think we may need more than one. Maybe three? One from each side and one from a birds-eye view."

Daisy suddenly jumped up from the bed. "Oh my gosh! Let's make them look like birds flying around. They can record not just our performance but the whole show!"

"That sounds so good," said Fifi. "Can you draw them that way Ewe?"

"I think so," said Ewe. "Daisy, please can you figure out the coding to make this work whilst I start to draw?"

"Gotcha," Daisy replied. She started working out codes and numbers, and plotting them down in a notepad, whilst Ewe drew.

"This is looking good guys!" said Danny, grinning at the screen that showed what Ewe was drawing. "Is that where the camera will be?" He stood up, pointing at the screen, however he stood up a little too quickly and hit his head on the hanging lamp shade. "Ow!"

"Danny, you keep forgetting you're extremely tall!" Fifi said. "Are you okay?"

"Yeah." He winced. "Ewe, can you invent an intelligent lamp shade that adjusts to heights?"

Ewe laughed. "Maybe one day, but for now, just duck!"

Ayo was sitting on the bed deep in thought. "Guys, I think I have some lyrics for the performance already. It's been playing in my head all day since we spoke about it. You know I can't sing but can I read it out?"

"Go for it," Ewe said. "Someone should film it, so we can practice."

"I'll do it," Daisy took out her mobile phone and turned on the voice recorder.

Ayo took a deep breath:

"We're all different people with so much to share.
We take care of each other because we care.
We choose to be happy and always to smile.
A smile goes a long way; it's always in style.

That's why Marshill is special and deep down we know.

That's why we'll celebrate come rain, shine or snow!

That's why we'll celebrate come rain, shine or snow!"

"Ayo that was brilliant!" Ewe said. Ayo blushed.

"Now, we just need someone with a good voice to help us with the tune and to sing it," Ayo said.

"We'll figure it out," said Ewe. "We need a performance name. Something that will really stand out."

"How about Beat Shakers?" asked Danny.

The girls pulled a face.

"What about Birdettes?" suggested Fifi. "That uses the theme and it's cute."

"Exactly! It's cute, like a girl group," Ayo argued.

"I agree. We need something that sounds vibrant," Daisy said.

"I got it!" Ewe said. "Stars of Paradise."

"Oh, I like that," Ayo said nodding slowly.

"Me too," agreed Danny.

"Perfect," Ewe said. "What's everyone doing this weekend? Maybe we can go to the community hall and practice?"

Everyone nodded in agreement.

"I'm starting to feel even more excited now," Daisy said. "Esi better watch out, she's got some competition!"

Chapter 4

Strops and Milkshake Shops

The friends made their way to the community hall on their repaired hoverboards, but they were surprised to see that it was full of other students practicing. Although it was nice to see that the competition had been received with such enthusiasm and excitement, it was also quite daunting–the different acts looked and sounded really good!

"Wow," said Daisy. "Did you just see that flip?"

"How did they do that?" Fifi asked, watching in awe.

"Look at Enzo!" Ayo pointed at the corner of the hall where their classmate was playing his drum kit like a professional.

Two students from the other Year Six class were rapping, as Enzo played the drums.

"I think it's really cool that different classes are working together," Danny said.

"They sound amazing. Do you think my song is good enough?" Ayo asked, looking worried.

"Ayo," said Daisy, turning to face him. "Your song *is* good enough."

Enzo and his friends had vacated the area, but as the group went to take their place, Esi appeared holding a portable microphone and small speaker.

"Okay guys, let's start with the song," Daisy said, taking out the lyrics from her pocket. "I'll try and sing it the best that I can."

Daisy took a deep breath, closed her eyes and sang out loud as best as she could, but Daisy was not the best singer and it came out a little croaky. "We're all different people with so much to sha–" She stopped mid-sentence, as she heard Esi loudly laughing into the microphone.

"Why are you laughing?" Daisy demanded. "Your microphone is on so I can HEAR YOU!"

The city community hall they used was huge but due to the number of performers, everything had an echo. Esi's laugh bounced around the entire room. Daisy felt like she was being laughed at from all directions.

Everyone looked at Esi in shocked silence.

"Just ignore her Daisy," said Fifi, shooting a dirty look at Esi. "She isn't worth you getting upset. You just need to keep trying and you *will* hit that note."

Fifi turned with her hands on her hips to face Esi. "It's not very nice that you laugh at people who are not as good as you. It's rude, Esi, and it's mean, and that's why people don't like you."

Esi was stunned. "Well," she began stiffly. "I shouldn't have done that Daisy. I'm sorry. You struggled because you need to sing in a lower key. Fifi, you're calling me mean, but you lot are always mean to me."

"No, we're not!" Ewe argued. "You never smile, you don't look happy and you make no effort with anyone."

"She's right. You always want to be alone and

never join in with anything," said Fifi. "So why would we hang out with you?"

"That's not true," Esi argued. "I do smile. You just never see me smiling. None of you have ever said a nice word to me. You must be jealous or something because I don't get it. It's not my fault that I'm gifted. It's funny how you can't see how intimidating you are when you walk around school in your big group."

Esi's eyes welled up. She angrily wiped the tears away before storming out of the hall.

"Great," huffed Daisy. "Now we're the bad guys."

"Daisy, did you see her starting to cry?" Danny asked, looking worried.

"Yes and I feel bad but it's not okay for her to laugh at me."

"This practice isn't going anywhere," Ayo moaned.

"I have an idea," Danny said. "And I promise we won't get into any trouble. Why don't we ask Esi to join us? Look at Enzo, working with people outside of our class. We should do the same. Plus,

Esi is a really good singer and we need someone to sing this song."

"Wait, you want Esi to sing with us?" Daisy frowned.

"I think she would be good for our group," Danny said.

"Hmmm." Ewe paced up and down room. Then her eyes lit up. "Danny is right! The aim of this is to work together. It would be a huge surprise to everyone if we had Esi in our group."

"What do you think Daisy?" Danny asked. Everyone turned to look at her.

Daisy didn't know how to feel. Esi was rude but she did make a valid point. They never invited her to do anything with them. Daisy always assumed it was because Esi liked being by herself, but maybe she was wrong.

Fifi placed her arm around Daisy's shoulders. "You don't have to do anything you don't want to do."

"It's no secret that I'm not a fan of hers, but I think it could be a good idea," Daisy said, making Danny grin. "We do need someone who can actually sing, but how can we get her to join us? She just stormed off!"

"Look, she thinks we're intimidating and we never invite her to hang around with us, so why don't we do that? Go round and see her, and ask her to hang out," Ayo suggested.

"Are we sure this is a good idea?" asked Fifi.

"I'm convinced she'll say yes if we ask nicely and apologise for being mean to her. Let's go to her house and talk to her. What's the worst that can happen?" Danny said.

Daisy groaned. She could think of a number of things that could go wrong!

"Okay." Daisy sighed.

"Let's get some milkshakes on the way from Mum's shop," Fifi said. "We can practice again tomorrow."

"Look at Danny,' said Ayo, pointing at Danny, who was already rushing out of the city community hall, with his hoverboard in one hand.

"That boy loves food so much!" Ewe laughed.

"That's probably why he's so tall," Ayo said, as they walked towards the exit.

It was true. Danny was the tallest boy in their school year.

Across the road, they could see Fifi's Mum's busy dessert shop.

Chapter 5

Unwanted Guests

Fifi's Mum made the best milkshakes in town, so many different flavours: chocolate brownie, strawberry, Oreo, birthday cake. Just one sip seemed to make all your problems go away.

Esi lived up the road from the shop, so as soon as they finished their milkshakes they headed to her house.

Danny took the lead and knocked on the huge wooden door with beautifully polished brass fixtures.

Esi opened the door, surprised to see her visitors. Her red eyes were a giveaway that she had been crying. Her tight ponytail, with perfectly formed ringlets, was now a mess around her shoulders.

"Hi." Danny waved.

"What do you want?" Esi said abruptly, stepping back from the door.

"We really want to move forward and try and make things work between us," Ewe said.

"So, you're here to apologise?" Esi asked.

Ewe glanced at Daisy and nodded at her.

"Yes," replied Daisy. "We're really sorry for being mean to you and making you feel left out."

Esi crossed her arms over her chest. "I already apologised, so I'm not going to again."

Daisy took a deep breath, trying to stop herself from getting annoyed.

"There's something not right about this," Esi said, eyeing them all suspiciously. "None of you have ever come round to see me before. So, who's going to tell me the truth about why you're really here?"

"Okay, okay, it was my idea," Danny said. "We did come to apologise, but there is something else."

"Well, what is it?" snapped Esi.

Daisy rolled her eyes.

"We would like you to hang around with us. Get to know us properly so we can be friends and maybe you can join us for the carnival talent show?" Danny said.

Esi's face turned from shock, to confusion, to anger in under five seconds.

"No!" Esi shouted. She slammed her door shut.

"I knew it! I told you she wouldn't want any part of this," Daisy said.

Fifi sighed. "I agree with Daisy. This is a waste of time. We really should be getting home and ready for practice tomorrow."

"Come on guys, let's try one more time," Danny pleaded. "I think you should do the talking this time Daisy."

"Me?" Daisy shrieked.

"She'll listen to you. Everyone does." Danny knocked on the door before Daisy could protest, then side-stepped, so Daisy was in front of the gang.

Esi opened the door. "Why are you still here?"

"Esi, I was hurt that you laughed at me while

I was singing, but we want to be friends and perform at the carnival together," Daisy said.

Esi's eyes widened. "You're actually being serious?" Daisy nodded. "I'm not sure about performing, but we can say hi at school."

"That sounds good." Daisy looked back at the group who nodded. "But please think about performing with us."

"I will, over the weekend." Esi said. She smiled at them, which transformed her entire face. "I'll see you at school."

They waved goodbye, as Esi shut the front door, more calmly this time.

No one was ready to go home just yet, so they jumped on their hoverboards and flew to The Hill, which was the highest peak at their local park.

"I have an idea," Daisy said, as they sat down on the grass. 'Hopefully this will show Esi that we're serious about trying to be her friend. Why don't we pick things to do that she likes? Then she'll see that we are making an effort."

"Good idea! Maybe we can start with asking her to lunch?" Ayo suggested.

"I think there's one more place we can take her for the wow factor?" Daisy said, glancing at Ewe.

"Where's that?" asked Ewe frowning.

"Your room! I think she'd love it and she can watch all our adventures on the EWE-TUBE."

"Yes! She can watch that video of us at the zoo, when we tried to blend in with the animals in our costumes and scared the life out of the zoo keeper," Fifi said.

"Or, the time we were on that magic carpet and we couldn't stop zooming around and Danny threw up," said Ayo, slapping his thigh and laughing.

"That was not funny," Danny huffed.

"You guys should really check the plans more carefully each time you make something," Fifi said, wiping away her tears after laughing so hard.

"Maybe she could get to see how much fun we have together and just how cool we are. Ewe, do you mind?" said Daisy.

"No, not at all," said Ewe. "Actually, talking

about things flying, maybe she can watch us finish the flying drone cameras?"

"Okay, so we have a plan?" Daisy looked at her friends who nodded in unison. "Bring on Monday."

Chapter 6

Operation D.O.G

On Monday they put their plan into action. The group did everything they could to spend more time with Esi and include her in their activities. On Tuesday, she sat with them at lunch, but didn't join in the conversation. On Wednesday, she played with them during playtime and joined in with their conversation at lunch. By Friday there was a shift. Esi was smiling and laughing with the group over their macaroni cheese.

Later that day, Esi was coming round to Ewe's house to see the Grape4D and EWE-TUBE. On the way out of school, Daisy pulled Ewe to one side.

"This is going good! I think we should talk

to her again about the performance when we get to yours."

"Good plan," Ewe said.

Esi's mouth dropped open when she stepped into Ewe's room.

"Whoa! I have never seen anything like this before. This is super cool!"

Ewe smiled. "This is where Daisy and I draw out our ideas and make them come to life."

"And they really do," said Fifi. "One time I wanted to know what my hair would look like in different colours and the girls invented this hat that changes your hair colour instantly. When I took the hat off and placed it back on my head, my hair colour went back to normal, but my dog chewed a bit of the hat without anyone realising and I had already picked green hair. When I put on the hat, to turn it back to normal, I had a strip of green hair."

"So that explains the green streak in your hair!" Esi said, staring at the neon green in the middle of Fifi's Afro hair.

Fifi laughed. "Yep, I got in so much trouble."

"We all got in trouble," Daisy corrected her.

"Right," said Ewe, rubbing her hands together. "Let's get to work finishing off the drone cameras."

Daisy picked up the notepad from the desk and sat beside Ewe in front of the Grape4D. Everyone else sat on the bed. They couldn't wait to see the bird of paradise drone cameras.

"What's a drone camera? And why do you need it?" asked Esi.

"We had this idea to film our performance at the carnival, so we can watch it later on the EWE-TUBE. We normally film all our adventures and watch them back, but this one is different, as we're all taking part. To make it more exciting, we're going to make the drone cameras look like flying birds of paradise and we'll film everyone else's performance from the sky," explained Daisy.

"Wow! That's such a good idea," Esi said, then she looked confused again. "What's EWE-TUBE?"

"I'll show you." Ewe handed Esi her tablet. "Pick any video."

Esi clicked a button and seconds later she

started laughing. "Wow, Daisy, I can't believe how high you got. That's so cool that you guys have this." Esi sighed. "It's a shame I won't be at the carnival this year."

There was an awkward silence. Ewe spun around in her chair with her eyes wide. "You're joking, right?"

"I wish I was," Esi said. "I can't make it because I'm a D.O.G."

"What do you mean you're a dog?" asked Daisy confused.

Esi laughed. "I'm a member of the Dream Opera Group, that's what D.O.G stands for. Twice a year, we go to different cities to help them rebuild play centres and then we perform a special song for them. I just found out that this year's D.O.G performance is on the same day as the carnival here at Marshill, so I can't make both of them."

Daisy looked deflated. "Is there anything we can say or do to make you choose the carnival over the D.O.G?"

"Well no, this year they're giving out an award

for the best singer and I'm doing a solo. The winner takes home the gold trophy."

"That sounds exciting," said Fifi. "It would have been nice to do the carnival together, since we're friends now."

"I know, I'm sorry guys. I would have loved to be part of your performance. I've really enjoyed hanging out with you all this week."

"Wait!" Daisy stood up. "What time is your performance?"

"About 11 o'clock in the morning, why?"

"The competition is at midday. If we're quick, I'm sure we can make it back in time."

"It's across town," Esi said. "We won't make it back in time."

"We can," Daisy said excitedly. "We'll get you to your D.O.G performance and to the carnival."

Esi frowned. "How?"

"Ewe and I can create a flying, erm, flying something that will help us get to the competition in time. I don't quite know yet."

"Okay," Ewe said slowly. "Maybe something like a flying carpet?"

Esi looked back at her new friends in disbelief and excitement. Could this really be happening? They were going to all this trouble, just for her?

"Wow guys! I can't believe your mission is to help me. If you can get me to both performances then I'm in. I used to think you were a bit weird," Esi blushed.

"Danny's a little weird," Fifi smirked. She ducked as he threw a pillow at her.

"I think you're all wonderful." Esi stood up and linked arms with Daisy. "Who cares about a little weirdness? I'll tell you a little secret. Singing opera and classical music is a bit boring to me, so I'm excited to join your performance. What's your stage name?"

"We're called Stars of Paradise," Daisy said.

"Nice name!"

"We're glad to help," Ewe said. "So, here's the plan for our performance. Fifi is going to help us design amazing costumes, Ayo and Danny will lead the breakdancing. We're all going to sing, but we're not the best singers and that's where you come in. Ayo already wrote some lyrics."

"Sounds good!" Esi said.

"And anyone who can't get the dance will just do a two-step." Ewe stood up and did two steps to the left, then two steps to the right, putting a bounce in between each move.

"Ooh! I can definitely do that," said Esi. "Have you choreographed any of the dance moves? I'd love to learn some."

"We've got something," said Ayo excitedly.

"Let's go to the garden and practice," Ewe said. "We can finish the drones later."

They stood in the middle of Ewe's garden where Danny positioned them in a star shape. Ayo said it would look good from a bird's eye view when they record the performance.

"Right step to the side and move your arms like you have wings," Ayo said. "But don't be stiff. It needs to look fun!"

They practiced the dance routine for half an hour and Danny added different positions and transitions. They all desperately needed a drink of water—dancing was a tiring job.

"Before we finish, can we please talk about

the costumes? I need to update my sister," Fifi. "We've got less than two months."

"Can I be a Goldie bird?" Esi asked.

"That would really suit you," said Fifi. "The gorgeous brown and gold feathers will really make your eyes stand out. We can even weave a gold braid through your hair."

"I'm going to be a Twelve-Wired bird," said Daisy. "I like the bold, black feathers mixed in with the bright yellow."

"I want to be the gold and brown Emperor bird," said Ayo. "My mum is going to help comb out my hair to make my Afro bigger, so it will look like a crown."

"I'm going to be the brilliant red and white King bird," said Danny.

"I'm thinking of being the multi-coloured, blue-beaked Magnificent bird," Ewe said.

"I'm going to be the green and red Splendid bird. I'll let Kim know. I can't wait to see us all dressed up," Fifi exclaimed.

Chapter 7

Is It a Bird or a Plane?

The next practice session at the community hall was a huge improvement from the previous session. The group had agreed to keep Esi's part a surprise, so although she was at practice, she sat on the side, watching with the rest of the students who came to watch the rehearsals.

They saw an improvement in every session. Daisy was sure she overheard Enzo say to Rueben, "They're the ones to beat," and he was looking right at them.

After another rehearsal, they went back to Ewe's house to sort out the transportation they would be using to get between the two shows.

"We need something to get us there fast," said Daisy.

"It needs to fly," said Ewe.

"We can use the codes we used for the updated hoverboards," Daisy suggested.

With that, Ewe began to draw the bird. It had four wings on either side with six seats, two huge exhaust pipes at the back, six flashing lights on the side, and a glass lid.

Ayo thought it looked like an underwater submarine with dodgy arms.

"This doesn't look right." He pointed at the screen.

Ewe tilted her head to the side to see it from Ayo's point of view. "But that's what makes them fly."

"But can't you make it look more like a paradise bird with maybe just two really big wings rather than four and lots of little feathers like the Raggiana bird?" Ayo asked.

"What does the Raggiana bird look like?" asked Ewe.

"It's the one that's green, yellow and brown, with long orange feathers."

"I think that could work Ewe, and you can still put three jet engines on each wing," Daisy said.

"What about music while we fly?" Danny said.

"Yes! With a popcorn machine?" Ayo said.

"Hmmm, I prefer candy floss," said Fifi.

"What about seatbelts?" said Daisy. "We need this to go really fast. As fast as the speed of light."

"You can do that?" Esi asked amazed.

Ewe carried on drawing and clicking away on her computer, while Daisy entered in the codes. After a few minutes, the girls looked at each other and smiled.

"Friends, I now present the Raggstar!" Ewe said proudly.

"Whoa," they all exclaimed.

They had created a magnificent bird of paradise that resembled the Raggiana bird but with a glass door on its back. The cockpit was the head of bird. It had beautiful orange wings, a bold green, yellow and brown body with fuchsia pink flashing lights, colourful seatbelts, an inbuilt music system, plus a popcorn and candy floss machine.

Daisy handed out the protective sunglasses. She

then pressed the black button and the Grape4D got to work.

They moved closer to the glass cabinet, almost sitting on top of each other, watching in amazement, as the Raggstar began to take shape. A rainbow of colours from the laser bounced around the glass cabinet. It was like a silent firework display. The Grape4D jerked backwards and forwards and then the Raggstar was born. It was beautiful, but too small.

"How are we supposed to all fit in?" asked Esi confused.

"There's some coding and a button I need to press before it blows up to its real size. I won't do it here," Daisy explained.

"We'll do it in the back garden," suggested Ewe. "Otherwise, we'll get in big trouble. Danny, can you please take one of the drone cameras with you? I think this will be a great opportunity to try it out." Ewe shoved a piece of paper in Daisy's hand. "Don't forget your codes." She then handed Fifi a mobile phone. "You and Esi can watch what Danny captures through the EWE-TUBE."

"I'm so glad I can do something to help," said Esi excitedly.

They headed to the back garden to test the Raggstar, tiptoeing down the stairs, to avoid disturbing Ewe's sister, Grace. She wasn't a big fan of their inventions. Unfortunately for them, Grace heard a creak on the stairs and paused from painting her nails. Blowing on her wet nails, she poked her head around the living room door.

"What are you up to?" Grace asked suspiciously. Her braids were tied up into a high bun.

"We're just going outside to take a look at something. Are you painting your nails?" Ewe asked sweetly, trying to distract her.

"I don't trust you or your friends. I know it's only going to lead to trouble, especially when you're all together."

"We're just going outside to test something we made," said Daisy innocently. "We won't be noisy."

"Hmmm." Grace stepped into the hallway. "What's that?" she asked, pointing at the Raggstar.

"It's our Raggstar."

"Your what? Wait a minute. Ewe, are you up to anything dangerous? Why do you have that bird?"

Grace had her arms crossed, with her fingers sticking out, so she wouldn't smudge her nails. The nail varnish hadn't yet dried and the smell wafted up Ewe's nose. She put her palms over her nose and looked back at Grace.

"Red nail polish and white, plush, new leather sofas don't really match, do they?"

Grace narrowed her eyes dangerously and Ewe smirked at her. They both knew they were not allowed to get anything on the new sofas.

"Whatever, Ewe," Grace snapped. "Just don't blow anything up. I have plans today."

Daisy and Ewe high-fived. They ran into the garden and Ewe placed the Raggstar on the grassy floor before motioning everyone to step back. They formed a semi-circle round Ewe.

"Right Daisy, put in the codes please," Ewe said.

Daisy began to type into the tablet as Danny flew the drone camera up above them.

"Okay, ready?" Daisy asked.

"Let's do it."

Daisy pressed the activation button on the side of the Raggstar. A sound escaped, as loud as thunder. The Raggstar rumbled, tumbled, bounced up and down and around the garden, like a bouncy ball. The fuchsia pink lights beamed. The exhaust pipes made a hollow drone sound. The feathers started to flap and the Raggstar began to grow.

Chapter 8

What Goes Up Must Come Down!

It didn't stop growing!

The Raggstar grew and grew, taking up all the space in the garden. The lights were flashing faster and brighter. The feathers were flapping more and more, knocking over the fence on both sides of the back garden.

"Oh no, Ewe, what's happened? It's massive!" screamed Esi.

"I don't know!" Ewe cried.

The Raggstar was still growing. The noise was deafening, making it difficult for them to hear each other.

"I must have put the codes in wrong," Daisy shouted, pulling out her notepad.

"Hurry up Daisy. We don't want to get blown away!" Fifi cried as she hid behind Ayo.

"This is so cool," said Danny, looking up at the Raggstar in awe.

"But I typed this in–" Daisy's voice trailed off, as the Raggstar cast a giant shadow over her.

"Oh no," gasped Ewe.

Daisy was frantically writing in her notepad. Esi and Fifi were looking from the Raggstar, to what was happening on the EWE-TUBE, and back to the Raggstar, in total disbelief. Only the boys seemed to be enjoying themselves, as they messed around with the drone camera.

"I've got it!" Daisy said, quickly typing into the tablet. "This should fix it. Okay, done."

At first, nothing seemed to happen but then, gradually, the Raggstar began to shrink in size, like a balloon letting out air through a tiny hole. The squashed fences sprang back into place as the Raggstar shrank back to its normal size.

Daisy fell to the floor looking exhausted. "That was close."

They were interrupted by Grace, who came

running into the garden. Well, she sort of waddled out like a duck–this time there were tissues between her brightly painted toes.

"Ewe! What was all that noise?"

Ewe blinked innocently. "I don't know what you're talking about Grace."

Grace looked around the garden. Nothing looked out of the ordinary, except for the strange colourful bird.

"What is that?" Grace asked, pointing at the Raggstar on the grass.

"Just a toy," Ewe said. "It's cool, isn't it?"

"No." Grace glanced at her wet nails. "I thought I heard something. Just don't do anything silly." She turned back and waddled back into the house.

"Right, shall we try it out?" Ewe asked.

They all jumped into the Raggstar.

"This is incredible! This is exactly what Ewe drew!" Esi said.

Inside the Raggstar it felt as though they were in a helicopter. There was a cockpit and designated seating for the pilot and co-pilot, who were Daisy and Ewe. Behind them were rows of seats with bright seatbelts and screens built into the headrests, so each passenger could see where they going. There was music playing out of the small speakers and the popcorn and candy floss machines were whirring away.

"Where are we flying to?" asked Danny, as he put on his seatbelt.

"We're going to the grounds where Esi will be performing, just to make sure we get there okay," said Daisy.

Ewe pressed a button and a map appeared on the dashboard. She used her finger to drop the location finder on the map.

"We're flying off in 5-4-3-2-1," Ewe said.

Whoooooooooooooooooosh!

Ewe closed her eyes as the Raggstar travelled so fast all the colours seemed to merge into one. They landed with a hard bump and Ewe slowly opened her eyes. They were in an empty field, but a few yards away, she could see a stage that had been built for the upcoming performance.

"I can't believe we're here," Esi said, peering

out of the window. "Look, that's the stage I'll be performing on."

"That was incredible!" said Ayo.

Daisy noticed Danny in the rear-view mirror, he was looking a little green.

"Danny, are you okay?"

"I need fresh air!" Danny moaned.

Daisy pressed the open button and the doors slid open. Danny jumped up and immediately kneeled over, throwing up his breakfast.

"I'll check on him," Esi said, taking off her seatbelt and jumping out of the Raggstar.

"I can't believe we did it!" Ewe said, giving Daisy a high five.

"I know! This is the best thing we've ever made."

Danny stood up, looking less green, but still not like himself.

"Can we go back?" he asked, sliding into his seat. Esi buckled him in. "I don't think I have anything left to puke up."

They took off and landed back in Ewe's garden. Daisy typed in her codes and the Raggstar became small enough to fit in the corner of Ewe's bedroom. Danny sat sipping a bottle of water, looking a bit better, as they practiced their routine. Knowing that they could get Esi to her show and get to the carnival in time seemed to give the group a new-found energy and they had the best rehearsal to date.

Chapter 9

Always On Time

The sounds of the carnival wafted over Marshill like a soft, summer breeze–the steel pans, the hustle and bustle of the floats, and stalls being put together. Barbeque and jerk chicken were cooking on the outside grills. Months of rehearsals had led to this wonderful day.

Fifi's sister, Kim, had created beautiful costumes for them. Each was unique and covered in sequins. She had also given them masks covered in bright paints and coloured gemstones. Esi was the only one in normal clothes. She was going to change after her first performance.

"I think you used all the sequins in Marshill." Fifi laughed.

"Ignore her, they look amazing. Thanks Kim." Daisy twirled her costume from side to side so that it caught the light.

"Just be careful or the sequins and gems will fall off," Kim instructed. She stood back and admired her work.

"We'd better get going," Ewe said, glancing at her watch, she had to keep everything running like clockwork today.

Fifi hugged Kim whilst Danny picked up the bag containing the drone cameras.

"Good luck!" said Kim, waving as she walked back towards her house.

Ewe placed the Raggstar gently on the floor and Daisy typed in the codes that would bring it to life.

The Raggstar rumbled and tumbled, jumped up and down, just like a bouncy ball. Then, the pink lights sparkled and the Raggstar transformed into the perfect size. They got in and buckled their seatbelts.

"Here we go guys!" said Ewe. "5-4-3-2-1."

Whooooooooooooooooooosh!

This time, Ewe kept her eyes wide open and she could see stars floating through the beautiful colours. Before she knew it they had landed in the same spot as last time but thankfully with a softer landing.

Daisy looked back at Danny, who was covering his mouth with both hands. She quickly pressed the door open and he ran out. They followed him out of the Raggstar. Daisy shrunk it back down and handed it to Ewe.

"Now, let's go and support Esi." Ewe grinned at Esi who smiled nervously.

"Let's do it," Danny said, smiling weakly. His face looked very pale.

They walked towards the stage. The closer they got, the more excited they were, except for Esi, who started to slow down.

"What's the matter?" asked Ayo, slowing down to Esi's pace.

"I'm a little bit nervous," she confessed.

"Really? I didn't think you ever got nervous," Ayo said surprised.

"I usually don't but I really want to win."

"You will and you'll have us cheering for you," Ayo said, putting his arm around her.

Esi smiled. She was starting to feel a lot better because she had her new friends with her.

They sat in the front row. Esi was called to the stage and given a microphone. She looked amazing in her red dress and when she sang her solo, the audience sat in silence, gazing at her. She sang beautifully and got a standing ovation! A few other acts followed, but none were as good as Esi.

Off stage, the children were getting lots of attention for their eye-catching costumes and were almost stealing the attention away from the D.O.G show. Danny had ventured off with Ayo to find some water and a paper bag to help with his motion sickness on the journey back.

"This is taking forever," Ewe said, looking at her watch. "We have to leave soon."

"I think this is the last act," Daisy said.

"I hope everyone likes our performance," Fifi said nervously.

"They will," Daisy said confidently, smiling at a little girl who was admiring her costume.

"Oh look," Ewe said. The host was walking onto the stage holding a red envelope.

"Thank you all for coming to the Dream Opera Group showcase. The talent today was just outstanding. I know everyone is anxious to know who the winner is, so without further delay." The host ripped open the red envelope.

Danny and Ayo ran back, eager not to miss the announcement. Daisy reached for Ewe's hand and squeezed it. Esi was staring at the envelope with her eyes wide.

"And the winner is. . . Esi Pendleton!"

Esi burst into tears as she was presented the golden trophy. Daisy and Ewe jumped up and hugged each other, as the crowd cheered loudly. They had to wait for a few minutes for Esi to reach them, as people kept stopping to congratulate her and admire the shiny, gold trophy.

"I can't believe it," Esi said when she finally reached them.

"You were amazing," Fifi said, hugging her.

"Wow," Danny said, touching the trophy.

Ewe glanced at her watch. "We have to go, or we're going to miss our performance."

"Oh, but I need to change," Esi said, looking down at her red dress.

"There's no time. You'll have to change there. Let's find some space so we can turn the Raggstar on."

They ran away from the crowds into an open space of fields. Ewe set the Raggstar on the floor for Daisy to type in the codes.

"Thank you guys," Esi said, looking at them with her eyes shining. "You're the best friends I've ever had."

"We're just glad we could help," Ewe

said. "Hopefully your good luck will rub off on us."

The Raggstar was ready to go. They hurried in and fumbled with the seatbelts. Ewe pulled up the map and placed the pin at the carnival.

"Everyone buckled up?" Ewe called.

"Yep!" Danny called from the back, waving his paper bag.

Ewe pressed the button to make the Raggstar fly, but nothing happened. She pressed it again, but still nothing.

"Daisy. . . help!"

"We're going to miss our slot!" Fifi cried from the back.

"One second," Daisy said, unbuckling her seatbelt. She reached for her notebook. "I wrote down a way to override the system if we ever had any problems."

She grabbed the tablet and typed in a long code.

"Okay, try now."

Ewe pressed the button and this time the Raggstar lifted from the ground.

"Daisy, you genius! Thank goodness you had a plan B! Carnival here we come!"

Chapter 10

Save The Best Until Last

The Raggstar landed on the grass with a thud, down the road from the carnival. This time the landing was smoother but poor Danny still reached for the paper bag. Daisy shrunk the Raggstar back down and placed it carefully in Danny's bag. Ewe handed Esi a bag containing her costume.

Esi glanced inside it and her eyes lit up. "What are those–"

"Sssh," Ewe said, winking at her. "It's a surprise."

They quickly ran down the street, laughing and shouting encouragement to each other, as they approached the entrance of the carnival. They ran over to Mr Tony and Ms Tori, who were looking worried, as they shuffled papers between them.

"Mr Tony, we're here," said Daisy, breathing heavily.

"I'm going to change," Esi said, running towards the toilets.

Mr Tony looked up and smiled in relief. "There you all are! We were worried you would miss your slot and wow, look at those costumes!"

"You're on first, which will give you a great chance to see everyone else's performance as well," said Ms Tori.

Ewe pulled out the cameras from Danny's bag. "Daisy and I made these drone cameras to capture the whole competition."

"Wow! You clever girls. What a thoughtful thing to do and they look spectacular."

"Thank you," Daisy said. She pulled out the remote control from the bag and handed it to Ms Tori. "Would you mind recording our performance please? It's really easy to control."

"I'd be delighted." Ms Tori smiled. "Everyone is going to love these cameras. They fit in perfectly with the theme." Ms Tori looked over Daisy's shoulder and frowned. "Esi, you're not down to perform are you?"

Esi looked amazing in her costume, even her trainers were covered in bright sequins with cool buttons on the side. She had the golden braid in her hair as Fifi had suggested.

"Not too loud Ms Tori, she's a surprise!" Daisy said.

"Ah," she said nodding. "A good one as well."

"Okay, you guys are up in a minute," Mr Tony said.

A young man, dressed in bright blue and carrying a microphone, hurried on to the stage that had been decorated like a jungle with fake plants, balloon trees and cardboard animals.

"Welcome to Marshill's annual carnival. My name is Alistair and I'll be your host for this year's show. We're going to start off the fun with performances from Marshill School. Please welcome the first act. . . Stars of Paradise!"

The audience cheered as the group made their way onto the stage. They put on their masks and stood in their positions. The bright lights came on showcasing their perfect star formation. The beat dropped and everyone stepped side to side as they sang Ayo's lyrics in perfect harmony.

Halfway through the song they stepped to the left of the stage and Esi walked down the middle like a model on a catwalk, belting out her solo. She took off her mask halfway through the song and the audience went crazy! Ayo and Danny broke into their breakdance routine with backflips and air freezes.

Ewe winked at Daisy who took out their secret weapon. Daisy pressed the button on the small remote and Esi's trainers began to light up. Esi looked down at them in awe and then she slowly started to hover above the stage. The audience were on their feet, clapping and cheering. Esi belted out a high note, while floating in the air, and then the lights dramatically went down.

"We did it!" Ewe said, punching the air. "Did you hear how loud they cheered for us?"

"Esi, I'm bringing you down," Daisy shouted. Esi gracefully floated back down to the stage.

"That was magical!" Esi said, grinning from ear to ear. "When did you come up with that?"

"Last night," Daisy said. "We wanted it to be a surprise for everyone."

The lights came on. Stars of Paradise removed their bird masks and took a bow before running off stage.

"You guys are the best!" Fifi said, grabbing them in a group of hug. "I never thought performing would be this much fun."

"You girls sounded great," Danny said.

"What about you and Ayo?" Esi said. "Your dancing was on another level."

"You really captured the spirit of this carnival," the host, Alistair, said, walking up to them. "That was incredible. You set the bar really high."

"Thank you." Ewe grinned. "I want to do it again and again!"

Alistair laughed. "I can't wait to see what the rest of the judges think about your performance. We've got a lot of acts to get through, so feel free to go and enjoy the carnival. The winners will be announced at the end of the day."

They stayed around to watch some of the other performances. Enzo's group was definitely their biggest competition because of the incredible dancing and drumming. Ewe double checked that their drone cameras were floating around the stage capturing everything before they walked around the carnival admiring their stalls and eating from the barbecue. There were so many beautiful costumes! It was amazing to see the effort everyone had put in.

Daisy saw her Mum, Dad and sister by the ice-cream van and she ran up to them, almost knocking over her Dad's ice cream in the process.

"You were incredible!" Mitsy said. "And look at your costume!"

"Didn't Fifi's sister do a great job?" Daisy swayed from side to side, showing off the gorgeous colours, to the delight of her baby sister.

"We're so proud of you," Alfred said. "I loved when that little girl was flying in the air! That must have been the work of you and Ewe."

"Yep!" Daisy said grinning.

"Hello fellow residents of Marshill! Can we

have all the performers to the stage?" Alistair called over the microphone.

"I'd better go," Daisy said.

"Good luck, darling," Mitsy said, kissing Daisy on the forehead.

Daisy caught up with her friends and they ran towards the stage. The Mayor was ready to announce the winner. He was wearing his trademark shiny, purple suit, holding a golden envelope in one hand and a large, shiny, gold trophy in the other.

"I'm so nervous," Esi said, biting her lip.

"Whatever happens, this was the best day of my entire life," Fifi said.

"Definitely," Ewe agreed.

"I just want to thank everyone for all their hard work in once again making the carnival a success," Mr Over said to a round of applause. "We have a special prize for the best performance; an all-expenses paid trip to see the wonderful birds of paradise in Paradise Bay."

"No way!" Danny's mouth dropped open.

"And the winners are. . ."

Mr Over ripped open the golden envelope. The friends held hands with their heads bowed and their eyes tight shut.

"Stars of Paradise!"

"Oh my gosh!" Daisy cried, jumping up and down.

"We won! We won!" Ayo said, doing a celebratory dance on the spot.

Ewe looked up to one of the drone cameras that was floating over them and blew a kiss to it.

"Can Stars of Paradise please come on to the stage?" Alistair asked.

Mr Over handed Daisy the golden trophy, which she hugged tight to her chest before raising it up high above her head, so everyone in the carnival could see. The crowd erupted into loud applause.

They were so excited about going to Paradise Bay together as a group! Already they could sense another adventure ahead of them.

It truly had been a magical day in Marshill, thanks to Daisy, Ewe and their wonderful friends.

About The Author

From designing shoes, developing her brand 'Mary Smith,' live singing, mentoring young women and telling stories to her nieces and nephews, Mary Obozua now adds 'Author' to the list. Mary grew up in a large family without a television. She credits this upbringing to stimulating her creative side, as she created stories to entertain her younger siblings. Inspired by the humorous relationship between her younger sister with her best friends, 'The Wonderful Life of Daisy and Ewe' was born and 'Stars of Paradise' is the first book in the series. She promises to bring girl power, a diverse cast, mystery and fun packed adventures to The WLDE series.